P9-DDP-535

Trail of Danger

BLAIRSVILLE SENIOR HIGH SCHOOL
BLAIRSVILLE. PENNA

Trail to Danger

Penn Mullin
AR B.L.: 3.5
Points: 1.0   UG

Cover Design and Illustrations: Tina Cash

Copyright ©1991, by High Noon Books, 20 Commercial Blvd., Novato, CA 94949-6191. All rights reserved. Printed in the United States of America. No part of this publication may be reproduced, stored in a retrieval system, or transmitted, in any form or by any means, electronic, mechanical photocopying, recording or otherwise, without the prior written permission of the publisher.

International Standard Book Number: 0-87879-912-5

09 08 97 96 05 04 03 02
9 8 7 6 5 4

You'll enjoy all the High Noon Books.
Write for a free full list of titles.

Contents

CHAPTER 1

A Call for Help

"Mark! Jason! Phone for either of you!" Mrs. Conway called.

"You take it, Jason. I'm beat," Mark said to his brother. He had just settled back on his bed to listen to some tapes.

Jason pulled himself up off the other bed and went to the hall phone. This better not be Ed wanting me to work at the deli this Saturday, he thought to himself. I just want to hang out this weekend.

"Hello," he answered. "This is Jason."

It was Bob Troy from the Youth Center. What could he want?

"Jason, we've got a real problem. I

wondered if you and Mark could help us out," Bob said. "You two know the back country so well and you've done these trips with me before. I had a backpack trip all set up for tomorrow. Taking ten kids from the city up the mountain to Sky Lake. But my two other leaders got the flu today. If I can't find people to take their places, we'll have to cancel the trip. And that will mean ten really disappointed kids."

"Right." Jason had a sinking feeling in his stomach. There wasn't going to be any way out of this one. He and Mark had owed Bob a big favor since last summer. And they did know the Sky Lake trail from other trips they had made with Bob. "Yes, I think we can do it, Bob." There goes hanging out and sleeping in this weekend, he thought to himself.

"You can? Terrific, Jason! You guys are great. Sorry this is such short notice. Can you be at the Youth Center by four tomorrow?"

2

"Sure. We'll be there," Jason told him.

"Just bring your backpacks and sleeping bags. I have all the food. And bring warm clothes. It might be cold up there," Bob said.

"OK. See you tomorrow!" Jason hung up and groaned to himself. Any other weekend but this one! He just wasn't ready for ten kids in the wilderness. Talk about work! But if he and Mark didn't go, the trip would be cancelled. And besides, they did owe Bob the favor.

"Hey, Mark!" he called to his brother. "I've got something to tell you!"

CHAPTER 2

Loading Up

"I can't believe we're really doing this," Mark said to Jason. They were in the car with their mother, driving to the Youth Center.

"Well, believe it. We're doing it. Let's just hope it's a good group of kids. Sky Lake's not a bad place for a trip. Wild country back in there, and beautiful. But I sure wanted to sleep late this weekend," Jason said.

"And I had planned to work on my bike," Mark said. "Oh, well, I can always do that next weekend."

"I think it's great you boys are helping Bob out," Mrs. Conway said. "He couldn't do the trip without you."

"Well, Bob's a super guy. Besides, we owe him a favor. Remember he wrote letters for us to win that backpack trip?" Mark asked.

"That's right. You needed a letter from someone that you had worked with in the wilderness," Mrs. Conway answered. "Bob must have written you a good one."

"I guess so," Jason said. "I couldn't believe we won. That was a super trip, one of the best we've ever had."

"Maybe you can teach these kids some things about backpacking. Sounds as if some of them have never been out of the city before," Mrs. Conway said.

"That's right. Hard to believe." Mark looked out the window. "They've never seen a forest or a mountain. We sure are lucky to live up here near the wilderness. Sometimes I guess we take a lot for granted."

"Here we are!" Mrs. Conway pulled the car into the Youth Center parking lot. A group of kids was standing around with their backpacks beside them.

"There's Bob!" Jason waved to a tall, thin, grey-haired man coming towards them.

"Marie, Mark, Jason, hi! Gosh, it's great to see you again," Bob said warmly. "Marie, your boys are sure terrific, helping me out like this." Bob started helping the boys unload their packs.

"Well, you helped them win that backpack trip, Bob. I think they're glad to be able to do this for you," Mrs. Conway said. "Have a great time and I'll see you Sunday night!"

The boys waved good-bye to their mother and then slapped hands together in the high-five sign. They followed Bob over to where the kids were standing by a small green bus.

Bob blew his whistle and everyone stopped talking. "Kids, I want you to meet your other leaders for this trip, Mark and Jason Conway. They're great backpackers and you can learn a lot from them. Now, if you kids will start getting on the bus, we'll load your stuff into the back."

The kids crowded onto the bus. Mark and Jason helped Bob load the backpacks and food boxes aboard.

"Some of these packs weigh a ton!" Mark said. "I wonder what the kids have in them."

"I gave each of them a list of what to bring when I handed out the packs last week. They know they've got to carry it themselves. But most of them have never carried—or seen—a backpack before. And they haven't any idea what five miles on a mountain trail means." Bob closed up the back of the bus.

"How many years have you been doing these trips, Bob?" Mark asked.

"This will be my tenth summer," Bob answered. "And I've loved it. It's such a great feeling to bring these city kids up here to the mountains. I've seen kids go through amazing

7

changes in just a weekend. You'll know what I mean when the weekend is over."

"Looks like a good group on this trip," Jason said. "Are they all about eleven or twelve years old?"

"Right. I don't think we'll have any problems. But you never can tell. Well, we'd better get going if we're going to make the campground before dark." Bob started towards the front of the bus.

"Are we going to camp at Grizzly Meadow?" Mark asked.

"Yes. We'll start hiking from there in the morning." Bob answered. "Oh, by the way, did you hear that the Silver Fox has been seen near Grizzly Meadow this spring?"

"The Silver Fox!" Jason couldn't believe it. The Silver Fox was an old man who lived alone in the mountains. Few people had ever seen him. No one knew where he came from. But once in awhile people would catch a look at him through the trees. And then he would be gone.

So the Silver Fox might be watching as they hiked, as they slept, all along the trail. Mark and Jason felt a chill go down their spines as they followed Bob onto the bus.

CHAPTER 3

Trouble Ahead

"We're off!" Bob started the bus and all the kids cheered.

Mark and Jason took seats near the back of the bus. That way they could keep an eye on the campers. Mark counted four girls and six boys. Tonight at the campfire he and Jason would learn all their names. Right now they were just a group of happy, excited faces.

"How long till we get there?" a curly-headed girl turned around to ask Mark and Jason.

"Only about an hour till Grizzly Meadow," Jason told her. "What's your name?"

"Marcy," she answered. Suddenly her face

had a troubled look. "But I didn't know there were grizzlies up there."

"Oh, don't worry, Marcy. There aren't any grizzly bears left around here. That name is just left over from a long time ago when those bears were up in these mountains," Mark said. "In fact, now there aren't any grizzly bears left in this whole state!"

"What happened to them?" Marcy asked.

"They were all killed off by hunters about a hundred years ago," Jason told her. "These days in our country animals are being protected so that their kind will survive. But back then no one cared about protecting the grizzlies."

"That's sad," Marcy said. "But I'm kind of glad there won't be any grizzlies up where we're going." She smiled and turned around in her seat.

"I think I'd rather have grizzlies sneaking around than the Silver Fox," Jason said to his brother. "Wouldn't you?"

"Yeah, I know what you mean. That really gives me the creeps, the thought of his watching us." Mark stared out the window into the woods. "I wonder who he is. And how long he's been in the mountains."

Suddenly someone started yelling in one of the seats ahead. A tall thin boy stood up in his seat.

"Give it back! Give it back!" he shouted at the smaller boy beside him.

"OK. OK. Here it is. I was just looking at it. No big deal," the smaller boy said.

Jason jumped up and went over to the boys' seat.

"What's the trouble here?" he asked.

"He stole my knife. Took it out of my jacket," the thin boy said. He was still standing, staring down at the smaller boy.

"It's OK now. You've got your knife back," Jason said quietly. "But you've got to close it up now. And sit down. What's your name?"

"Carl." The boy closed the knife and sat down. His eyes were dark with anger.

"Maybe I'd better hold onto that knife for awhile, Carl. You can talk about all this later with Mr. Troy." Jason reached out for the knife. Carl silently put it into his hand and looked away.

"Now, what's your name?" Jason asked the boy beside Carl.

"Bryan. I didn't steal his knife. I was just looking at it." His voice sounded scared. "Honest I didn't."

"OK, don't worry. It's over. We'll be up at the campsite soon." Jason started back to his seat.

Suddenly Carl stood up and pushed past Jason as he went towards a seat at the back of the bus.

Jason had an uneasy feeling as he sat back down beside his brother.

"That's one unhappy kid," Jason said to

Mark. "There could be some problems on this trip."

"I sure hope you're wrong, Jason. But I know what you mean," Mark told him. "I think there's trouble ahead."

CHAPTER 4

Grizzly Meadow

"Hey, look! We're coming into Grizzly Meadow! That sure was fast," Jason said.

Bob parked the bus and stood up to talk.

"We're here, everybody! Welcome to Grizzly Meadow," Bob said. "When you get off the bus, take your packs and put them under the trees. Lay out your sleeping bags where you want them. Then you can help Mark and Jason find firewood for cooking dinner."

Kids started getting off the bus. Carl brushed by Mark and Jason without looking at them.

"Wow, I'd forgotten how great this place is," Jason said as they got off the bus. They were surrounded by tall pine trees, and the air felt cool and fresh on their faces. Out beyond the trees was Grizzly Meadow, a large green open field.

Mark and Jason started helping Bob unload the bus. Kids came and picked up their packs.

"Saw you had some trouble back there with Carl," Bob said.

"Yes. Not good. He's an unhappy boy." Jason handed Bob the pocketknife. "I told him you would talk with him later."

"Do you know much about Carl?" Mark asked.

"Not much. Only that he's had a hard life," Bob answered. "He's switched schools a lot. Been in trouble a few times. I know I'm taking a chance bringing him along. But maybe we can help make some good things happen for Carl up here. Getting him to feel good about himself would be an important first step."

"Right. We'll hope there's a way to make that happen," Jason said.

"Well, I'll get started on dinner." Bob picked up one of the food boxes. "See if the kids need any help getting their sleeping bags set up. Then they can bring me some firewood. I'm making chili tonight!"

"Oh, great! I remember it was terrific," Mark said. "I can't wait!"

The kids were busy undoing their bags. Some already knew about putting a plastic groundcloth down first and then the rubber pad for under the sleeping bag. Mark and Jason showed the others how to set it up. The boys had all grouped together in one place. The four girls were setting up their bags over by a bunch of huge boulders.

Mark and Jason noticed that Carl had not yet unrolled his sleeping bag. He sat on the ground beside it.

"When do I get my knife back?" he asked

when the boys walked over to him.

"When Bob says it's OK, Carl," Jason answered. "Need some help getting things set up here?"

"I can handle it," Carl said and looked away.

"Hey, where's my firewood?" Bob called out. "Get busy if you want dinner, kids!"

Kids started running around picking up pieces of wood. Carl just kept sitting there by his pack. Mark and Jason decided to just leave him alone for now.

Soon Bob had a huge fire going.

"I'll let this burn down to a nice bed of coals. Then I'll put on my pot of chili," Bob said.

"We'll get the kids started on the fruit salad." Mark and Jason set out apples, oranges, grapes, and bananas on the picnic table. Then they helped the kids cut these up and fill a huge bowl. Mark unpacked the cornbread Bob had brought up from the Youth Center.

"Boy, I'm hungry!" Marcy said. "That chili sure smells good!"

Bob had put the pot of chili on the coals. Kids got out their tin cups and plates and sat around the fire to wait. The campground was beginning to grow dark now. The wind rustled the tops of the tall pines overhead.

Carl still sat alone, away from the fire.

Mark and Jason saw Bob looking over at Carl every now and then. They knew he was worried about the boy. Maybe food would bring Carl over to the group.

Bob leaned over to taste the chili. "It's ready! Come and get it!" he called.

The kids lined up while Bob, Mark, and Jason dished out chili, cornbread, and fruit salad. There was a big jug of lemonade on the picnic table, too.

Bob fixed a plate of food and took it over

to where Carl sat. Mark and Jason watched him sit down beside the boy and offer him the food. But Carl wouldn't take the plate or even look at Bob.

"This may be one of Bob's toughest cases," Jason said. He and Mark sat down and started on their chili. Bob fixed himself a plate and came over to eat with the boys.

"I just wish I could get him to talk to me," Bob said as he sat down. "I told him I wanted to talk to him about the knife. But he just sat there."

Mark and Jason could tell Bob was worried. Maybe he was afraid that Carl might run away. Trying to find him up here in all this wilderness was a thought that made the boys shiver inside.

After cleanup time and a marshmallow roast, it was bedtime.

"Don't keep any candy or gum in your sleeping bags, kids," Bob told the group. "Give it to me to lock up in the bus. Bears love candy, and I wouldn't want us to have any unwelcome visitors tonight!"

Mark and Jason helped the kids get settled in their sleeping bags. Marcy looked very worried when Jason checked on her.

"I'm scared somebody's hiding candy in their sleeping bag and not telling. Then the bears will come," she said.

"Don't worry, Marcy. I think everybody feels the same way you do. Nobody wants bears coming into our camp. You just go to sleep and it will be morning before you know it," Jason told her.

"Well, OK. Night." Jason watched the top of her curly head disappear down into the sleeping bag.

Carl had unrolled his bag and gotten into it. He had pulled the top of the bag up over his head and now lay very still.

"Night, Carl," Mark said as he walked past

the boy. There was no answer.

Mark and Jason got into their sleeping bags. From where they lay they could watch the cozy flickering light of the campfire. They could hear the soft happy whispering of the campers as they drifted off towards sleep.

"Well, that's one sleepy bunch of kids."

Soon Bob came over and started getting into his sleeping bag.

"Well, that's one sleepy bunch of kids," he said.

"Was Carl still awake?" Mark asked.

"He wasn't talking. I wish I knew what was making him so angry. I think it's more than just the knife problem. Maybe something happened at home right before he came. Well, let's hope tomorrow is better," Bob said. "Sleep well, boys. And thanks again for coming along this weekend."

"That's OK, Bob. We're glad we came. You sleep well, too."

The boys lay in their sleeping bags looking up at the thousands of stars in the night sky. The wind made a sound like soft rain in the tall pines above their heads.

"I keep thinking about the Silver Fox," Jason said. "That he's maybe somewhere out there watching us right now."

"I know what you mean," Mark answered. "And we'd never know it if he was. There's so much blackness out there."

Somewhere in the distance two owls called softly to each other in the night stillness.

CHAPTER 5

Something in the Night

"Mark! Jason! Time to get up!" Bob was waking them. It was just barely light. The kids had not woken up yet. Mark and Jason checked Carl first thing. He was still there, curled up in his sleeping bag.

"So far, so good," Mark said.

Jason thought for a moment. "I think we had better keep an eye on him today just the same," he said.

The boys knew Bob liked to get up early to talk about the day's plans. After washing up, they helped Bob start a fire.

"No bears last night," Bob said. "Or if they were here, they didn't do any damage. But something woke me in the night." Bob blew gently on the growing fire. "I'm not sure what it was. But I had the strangest feeling someone—or something—was here in camp, watching us."

Jason felt a chill go down his back. "The Silver Fox?"

"I don't know. But there was something here last night." Bob stood up.

"Would there be any footprints?" Mark asked.

"I checked. Too many pine needles on the ground." Bob added some pieces of wood to the fire.

"Would the Silver Fox ever try to steal food?" Jason asked Bob.

"No, I don't think so. There's never been a report that he's stolen anything. But few people ever see him. He's fast and he knows these mountains well," Bob said. "I wish I could meet him sometime."

Mark and Jason helped Bob unload the breakfast food from the bus.

"After breakfast we'll divide up the food for today and tomorrow among our three packs. You remember the trail to Sky Lake. It's not a hard hike. About six miles. The kids will feel so proud of themselves when they've done it." Bob started mixing up pancake batter.

"That's a pretty narrow trail in spots, isn't it?" Mark asked.

"Right. We'll have the kids hike in single file. You be in the middle, Jason, and you bring up the end, Mark," Bob told the boys. "Let me know if any kids are getting too tired. This is the first big hike for most of them. They all should be able to make it OK. They're in pretty good shape."

"OK. Sounds good," Mark said. "And let's hope things work out with Carl today."

All the kids were soon lined up for pancakes. Mark and Jason were surprised to see Carl had joined the line.

"The day's already looking better," Jason said to his brother.

After breakfast Bob called all the kids together.

"Before you get your packs ready, I just want to tell you about our hike today. It's about six miles long. It will be steep in some places. You'll get hot, so be sure to fill both your water bottles here in the camp sinks. Don't ever drink the water in the stream or you might get sick. If you get too tired, tell Mark, Jason, or me, and we'll take a rest stop. Any questions?"

"How long will it take us?" Bryan asked.

"That depends on you kids." Bob smiled. "But I bet we'll make Sky Lake in time for a nice long swim this afternoon! Now, get your packs ready. Then we'll do a camp check to make sure we've left a clean campground. That's one of the first rules of camping. It was

28

clean when we got here. We want to be sure it's just as clean when we leave."

Mark and Jason helped the kids get their packs ready. Each pack was made up of a large knapsack attached to a metal frame. The rolled-up sleeping bag fit under the knapsack part. Getting the bags rolled up small was a big problem for some of the kids.

Finally everybody was ready to leave.

"One last thing," Bob told the group. "One of our most important rules is that you don't ever leave the trail unless we tell you it's OK. Now, we're ready to start. You left a very neat campground. I'm really very proud of you. Here we go!"

The kids followed Bob in single file. Carl was last in line, next to Mark. He kept his head down and looked at no one. As they left, Mark turned around to take a last look at the campground. Suddenly he thought he saw someone there under the trees. Or were his eyes playing tricks on him? This Silver Fox idea has you spooked, he told himself. He turned and followed the line of hikers. But he knew he would be looking behind him all along the trail.

CHAPTER 6

Danger on the Rocks

It was getting hot. The sun blazed down on the hikers as they climbed the steep trail. They had left the forest behind now and were going higher up into the mountains. The trail dropped off steeply on one side. Anyone who fell would roll a long way down to the rocks below. The kids walked slowly and carefully.

"I can't wait till we swim in the lake. I'm so hot," Marcy told Jason.

"Me, too. Bob will call a rest stop soon. We could all use a drink of water," Jason said. "You're all doing great."

The trail led into a group of trees. Everybody sat down in the shade and opened the water bottles. Carl still sat away from the group, quiet and unsmiling.

"How much farther is it?" asked Kevin, one of the younger boys.

"Well, we've still got a ways to go yet. Maybe four miles," Bob told him. "We'll stop for lunch soon. You guys are making good time."

"Hey, Bryan's gone!" one of the kids cried.

"He wanted to climb up on those big rocks." Marcy pointed up towards a huge bunch of rocks above the trail.

Mark ran over towards the rocks. "Hey, Bryan!" he yelled. "Time to go. Come on down!"

There was no answer. He yelled again.

Then they heard something. The soft sound came from somewhere up in the high rocks.

"He's in trouble!" Bob yelled. "There he is! I can see him. He's stuck on that ledge between two rocks. He can't turn around. Mark, Jason, let's go after him!"

Suddenly one of the kids started running towards the rocks. It was Carl! He had taken off his pack and was starting to climb. Jason started to call out to him to stop.

"No. Let him go," Bob said.

Mark and Jason stood with Bob and watched Carl move like a spider up into the rocks. His hands and feet found holes in the steep rock walls as he moved quickly towards Bryan on the ledge.

"Where'd he learn to climb like that? He's a regular Spider Man!" Jason watched Carl in amazement.

"Around home that's what they call him, too!" a small boy named Dan told them. "Spider Man. He can go from one apartment house to the other so fast. Jumps from roof to roof. And he can climb anything."

Carl had reached Bryan now. He was beside him on the narrow ledge. Carl reached out to touch Bryan's arm and said something to him. Bryan slowly started to move back along the ledge towards Carl. Carl held onto his arm and Bryan came towards him.

Mark and Jason held their breaths. If Carl and Bryan fell now it was a long way down.

Carl had reached Bryan now.

34

All of a sudden Bryan stopped. Carl said something to him. Then Bryan began to move again. Slowly. Finally he reached the end of the ledge. He was safe! Everybody cheered. Carl and Bryan stepped down off the rocks. They slapped hands in the high five sign before they started back towards the group.

"I can't believe it," Jason said to Mark as they watched Carl and Bryan coming down. "This is terrific!"

"Pretty amazing stuff. I'm glad Bob stopped us from going up after Bryan," Mark said.

Bob was running towards Carl and Bryan. He put an arm around each boy and hugged him hard. His smile stretched from ear to ear. Then he pulled each boy off to the side for a moment and talked with each of them alone.

Then the kids came rushing up. "Hey, Carl. You sure can climb. Hey, Spider Man!" Carl smiled and laughed as the kids crowded around him. Bryan stuck right by Carl's side.

"Give me five, Carl," Jason said when he finally could get close to the boy.

"And me, too!" Mark said, putting out his hand. "Great work, Carl. What a rock climber!" Carl slapped hands happily with Mark and Jason. "Hey, thanks," he told them.

"OK, everybody. We'd better get moving," Bob called out. Then he came over to Mark and Jason. "Boy, am I happy! Carl's proud of himself and feels great. Do you know what he told me? Someone at home had called him chicken for not wanting to start in a new school next year. He didn't like thinking of himself as scared. But he didn't know what to do about it."

"Was that why he was acting so angry?" Jason asked.

"Yes. But now, after doing this brave thing, he feels good about himself again. We talked about that it's OK to feel scared about something like changing schools. It's not anything to be ashamed about."

"I guess I'm secretly glad Bryan got himself stuck up there," Mark said.

"I'm glad—and not secretly," Bob laughed. "Come on, let's get these kids up to Sky Lake!"

CHAPTER 7

Signs of Danger

The lunch stop was beside a beautiful waterfall. The icy water felt wonderful to the kids as they took off their hiking boots and went wading.

Bob called Mark and Jason over to where he stood along the stream. He pointed to some large tracks in the mud.

"Bear tracks," Mark said.

"Yes, big ones. This doesn't look like our regular black bear track." Bob sounded worried. "These look like grizzly tracks."

"But they couldn't be!" Jason stared at Bob. "There aren't any grizzlies left in this whole state!"

"That's what we thought. But here are the tracks," Bob said.

"Aren't grizzlies a lot more likely to attack humans?" Mark asked. He felt a chill go down his back.

"Yes. They don't have the same fear of man that the common black bears do. I don't like the idea of a grizzly being anywhere around us. I should probably take the kids back down the mountain," Bob said. "But I hate to disappoint them when they've come so far. We'll just be really careful about keeping them close to camp tonight. And we'll keep a fire burning all night long."

"How do you think a grizzly ever got up into these mountains? It would have to travel hundreds and hundreds of miles," Jason said.

"Maybe it's always been here, and no one's ever seen it. Maybe there are more of them. It's a mystery. And not one I like," Bob started to walk back towards the group of kids. "Watch for more of these tracks as we go. But keep it quiet."

"Right," Mark answered. He and Jason were filled with a creepy feeling as they started up the trail again. The mountain seemed full of unknown, hidden things. First the Silver Fox . . . and now a grizzly.

"Sky Lake is just on the other side of this forest," Bob called out to the kids. "Not much farther now. Think of a swim in that nice cool water!"

Some of the kids were starting to complain about how heavy their packs were feeling. Mark and Jason were busy keeping the kids going for the last mile. But they couldn't help watching the dark forest around them. Was a huge silver-furred grizzly silently watching them through the trees? And the Silver Fox? Was he watching them, too?

Suddenly the trail came out into bright sunlight, and there before them was beautiful

Sky Lake. There were white sandy beaches all along its shores. Deep green pines surrounded it. It was like a bright blue jewel hidden among the mountains.

The kids dropped their packs at the campground and got out their swim suits. Then they ran for the lake with Mark and Jason following them. Bob stayed behind in camp.

Sky Lake felt deliciously cool on everyone's hot, tired feet as they waded out on the lake's smooth sandy bottom.

"I'm glad Bob makes everybody pass a swim test before they come on his trips," Mark said.

"Right. Makes our job easier." Jason turned to look back at the shore. Something white caught his eye. It was moving among the trees.

"Mark, this is creepy. I thought I saw something—or someone—watching us from those trees."

"Probably Bob," Mark said.

"Or the Silver Fox! I keep thinking about him."

"Relax. He's probably miles from here. Come on! Let's swim out to the kids."

Jason followed his brother out into the lake. But he couldn't forget what he had seen. Someone was there watching them through the trees. And somehow Jason knew it was not Bob.

CHAPTER 8

Night Watch

Dinner was over and darkness was coming on fast. Sky Lake was still and peaceful now. And there was a soft pink glow in the sky left behind by the setting sun. Along the dark lake shore the one spot of brightness was a huge campfire among the trees.

"I want to keep the fire going all night long," Bob was telling Mark and Jason. "We'll take turns sitting up on watch."

"Should we put all the food up on a bear string?" Jason asked.

"Yes. I found a good tall tree down by the lake," Bob answered. "Let's tie up our food in these bags and then put them up in the tree when the kids go to bed. No sense worrying them about the grizzly."

That's for sure, thought Jason. After all, I told Marcy there were no grizzlies around here.

The boys helped Bob fill the bags with packages of food. Then they pulled each bag closed with the strings at the end.

The kids were starting to sing songs around the campfire. Firelight flickered softly in their faces. It was hard to believe there could be anything dangerous in a night like this. Mark and Jason sat down and joined in the singing. They watched as Bob took a seat next to Carl by the fire. The boy looked happy and contented. There was no more anger in his face.

"Did Bob tell you he's going to try to get Carl in a rock climbing class this summer?" Mark asked his brother.

"Hey, that's super! Carl will be teaching the class before long," Jason laughed.

Soon it was time for bed. Mark and Jason made sure the campers were in their sleeping bags. Then Mark followed Bob down to string up the food while Jason stayed behind with the kids.

Bob had chosen a tall pine with a long thin branch sticking out to the side. He had thrown a rope over this branch before it had gotten dark. Now he and Mark tied the food bags to both ends of this rope. With another rope, they pulled the food bags up into the air about fifteen feet above the ground.

"Now let's see any grizzly try to get that!" Bob chuckled. But Mark knew the older man was worried about the danger of a grizzly in the night.

Bob and Mark walked back towards the campfire. Behind them, the two dark food bundles swung slowly in the night wind.

Jason was putting more wood on the fire.

"OK if you take the first watch?" Bob asked

him. "Mark can take over at midnight. Then I'll take from three o'clock on. Those are the hours when I'm most worried about that grizzly coming around."

Jason sat down beside the fire and pulled a blanket around his shoulders. The kids were sleeping close in to the fire tonight. He could see some of their sleeping faces in the firelight. Somewhere in the distance an owl hooted softly. And the wind rippled through the trees above his head. He listened hard to the night sounds around him. From time to time he added more wood to the fire. And he thought about the grizzly that was maybe out there in the darkness beyond the fire. And the Silver Fox. Jason had asked Bob if he had been watching the swimmers from the shore. Bob had said no.

Jason's eyes burned with tiredness. Could he stay awake till midnight?

Suddenly Mark was shaking him! "Jason!

Wake up! I'm taking over."

"What? Oh, no! How long have I been asleep? Did anything . . . ?"

"Everything's OK. Don't worry. Go ahead and go back to sleep." Mark began putting wood on the fire to build it back up.

Jason stumbled over his sleeping bag. He was asleep again almost instantly.

Mark sat watching the fire as it began to crackle brightly. No bears would dare to come into a camp where there was a fire like this burning. He just had to keep it built up. It couldn't be allowed to die down. Mark kept feeding the fire more wood. The forest around him was quiet except for the soft wind in the high branches.

"My turn." Mark jumped as he felt Bob's hand on his shoulder. "Everything OK?"

"Sure. Pretty quiet. Gosh, the time went by fast!" Mark answered.

"It's three a.m. You go get some sleep

now," Bob told him.

Mark went over to his sleeping bag and lay down. The last thing he saw before his eyes closed was Bob sitting there quietly, staring at the fire.

CHAPTER 9

A Time to Choose

Jason didn't know what woke him. He sat up straight in his sleeping bag. The sky was just beginning to turn light. He looked at the fire. It had gone out. Where was Bob? Somehow he knew something was wrong. He shook his brother's shoulder.

"Mark, wake up! I think something's wrong! I don't see Bob and the fire's gone out. Remember? He said it was important to keep the fire going. He wouldn't have let it go out."

"What? Bob? Probably took a walk. Go back to sleep," Mark mumbled.

"No." Jason got to his feet. "I'm going to look around."

He headed towards where they'd hung the bear string. Maybe Bob was getting the food down. Now he heard Mark running behind him down the trail.

Suddenly they both stopped. They froze. A huge bear was ripping apart the food bags on the ground. And Bob lay close by with blood all over his face. The grizzly had come. They had never seen such a huge animal in their lives.

Mark and Jason could barely breathe. Their hearts pounded wildly. Was Bob alive? They were still too far away to see if he was conscious. Would they have a chance if they ran? But if they ran, would they lead the bear to the sleeping kids? They had to do something—but what?

The grizzly kept ripping at the food bags with his long sharp claws. They watched him cramming the food into his mouth—eggs, bacon, sugar. It was a horrible sight. And Bob lay there only a few feet away. Would the bear start on him next? The boys watched, frozen with fear. Soon the bear would smell them.

Maybe Bob is playing dead, Jason suddenly thought. That's what you were supposed to do if attacked by a grizzly. Please be alive, Bob, please, Jason said to himself.

A huge bear was ripping apart the food bags on the ground.

Suddenly the bear stopped ripping at the food. He swatted at the empty bags with his deadly claws. Then he moved towards Bob. The boys watched in horror. Suddenly they both knew what they had to do.

"Hey! Hey! Yah! Yah!" they screamed at the grizzly and jumped up and down. Surprised, the bear looked up and saw the boys for the first time. Then he started toward them. The closer he got, the bigger he looked.

"Run!" screamed Mark.

They knew they couldn't run towards camp. They raced wildly through the woods. Their chests felt as though they would explode. They could hear the grizzly crashing through the woods behind them. Any minute they would feel his terrible claws. On and on they ran. Suddenly they knew the crashing had stopped. Was the grizzly only trying to trick them into thinking he had gone? They had to be very careful.

"Take another way back. We've got to get to Bob," Mark panted.

The boys circled around and slowly crept back to where they had seen Bob. Would they find that the grizzly had returned to finish him off?

They stopped. Something was moving. A man was kneeling beside Bob. They ran towards him. The man looked up at them. His hair was silver white, and his tanned face was deeply lined. The Silver Fox. The boys did not need to ask who it was. All they knew was they were very glad to see someone.

"He's in pretty bad shape," the man told them. "He's in shock from losing a lot of blood. But I've got the bleeding stopped for now." He was pressing down with a bandana on a huge gash in Bob's shoulder. He seemed to know just what to do.

Bob was unconscious. His face was a mass

of bloody cuts and scratches. His skin was a terrible grayish color.

"Run back to camp and get a sleeping bag and your first aid kit. We've got to keep him warm and take care of these cuts. One of you stay with the kids. That bear's still around. And mad. I went after him with a torch." He pointed to a huge stick that lay still burning on the ground.

Mark and Jason raced back to camp. Mark brought back the sleeping bag and first aid kit. Jason stayed with the kids. They all wanted to know what had happened. Jason tried not to alarm them. He did not say anything about the bear. He just said that Bob had been hurt and that Mark and an older man were taking care of him. He tried not to let them see how worried he was and kept them busy playing games.

The Silver Fox was gently washing the cuts on Bob's face with cold water. Mark helped him carefully roll Bob into the sleeping bag. Then the Silver Fox took a tube of disinfectant from the first aid kit and touched each cut on Bob's face.

"We've got to get him to the hospital. I can't tell how much blood he's lost. One of you boys will have to go down the mountain for help. Tell the rangers at Grizzly Meadow to send up a helicopter. I'd better stay here in case the bleeding starts again," the old man said. "And in case the grizzly comes back."

"I'll go down. My brother will stay with the kids," Mark said. "Sir, thanks—for what you've done for Bob, and for stopping the grizzly. We would never have made it without your help."

"You boys did a brave thing. You were pulling that grizzly away from Bob and the kids, weren't you?"

"Yes. We had to. Sir, quickly, can I ask—you're the Silver Fox, aren't you?"

The old man smiled. "Well, is that what they call me these days? Sounds too elegant." He looked down at his faded tan shirt and jeans. "Hey, you'd better get along. Be fast and careful. I'll do the best I can for Bob. He's a good man. Loves these mountains like I do."

"But how do you know . . . ?" Mark started to ask. And then he understood. "I'll go tell my brother I'm going. Be watching for that chopper—soon!" Mark waved at the Silver Fox as he ran back towards camp.

Without a pack and a line of kids, Mark made it down the trail in less than three hours. The rangers radioed the paramedics in town to send up a helicopter. It first landed in Grizzly Meadow to pick up Mark. Then it swung up into the mountains. Mark's chest felt tight with fear for Bob. But he felt an excitement, too— and hope. Maybe it was because the Silver Fox was there with Bob.

"There's the lake now," the pilot said. "Show me where to put this thing down, Mark."

The helicopter lowered itself towards the clearing. Mark watched the figures of the Silver Fox and Bob grow closer and closer. Please, let Bob still be alive, he prayed.

The paramedics jumped out of the helicopter as soon as it touched down. Mark followed them as they ran towards Bob.

"He's still hanging in there," the Silver Fox told the paramedics. "He's one strong man. And you're one fast hiker," he told Mark. He stood up and put his arm around Mark's shoulder. "Thanks." Then he started off towards the woods.

"But you're not leaving!" Mark said to him. "Please, stay here for awhile. There's so many questions we want to ask you and . . . "

"You and your brother love these mountains. We'll meet again. I'm certain of it." The Silver

Fox waved and turned back towards the woods. Mark watched him until he disappeared among the trees.

Suddenly Mark heard Jason's voice and the sound of the kids coming to wave good-bye to

The Silver Fox waved and turned back towards the woods.

Bob. Today Bob was going down the mountain for the first time without a group of kids behind him. Mark knew that he and Jason would take over for Bob on this trip down.

He remembered a phone booth near where the bus was parked. They could call the Youth Center to send someone to drive the bus back. And Mark knew there would be nothing to fear along the trail. The Silver Fox would never be very far away.